# TOCCATA OBBLIGATO
## *Serenading Kyra*

**By**

**Jennifer Theriot**

Toccata Obbligato—
Fast moving, lightly fingered virtuosic passages of music
indispensable in performance.

# TODD O'MALLEY- ROCK GOD OR ASS WIPE? THE VERDICT IS STILL OUT...

**FUCK WAD. MOTHER FUCKER. ASSHOLE. ASS WIPE. CONCEITED. FULL OF** yourself. You name it, I've been called it. On the other hand, I have been told: "Oh my God! You look exactly like Adam Levine." "You're a rock god." "You've got a Prince Albert? Can I see it?" Or my all-time favorite, "That was the best sex I've ever had!"

I'm Todd O'Malley and my life is, or was, pretty fucked up. You all probably already know that I play lead guitar in a band called Avenue, and I'm from Highland Park, Illinois. In addition to guitar, I also play keyboard and I'm pretty badass on the drums.

I've never been on the short end of getting my lights fucked out. The women are plenty, and I've had my share of them. Looking back, and I'm not really proud of it now, but I can boast that I've been in a ménage à trois on more than one occasion. At the time it was pretty fucking incredible. One chick even videoed it, which eventually came back to bite me in the ass. More about that later, folks.

So I'm gonna let you in on a little secret. Sometimes I feel so alone. Are you shocked? I know you're probably thinking, 'How can a guy who has everything feel lonely?' I can have sex anytime I want, but it gets really old. After a while, a hole is a hole is a hole.

Lately I've been just coming home alone after the shows. I'll have a few beers before I go to bed and rely on writing music as my outlet. I'm tired of the hassle with chicks. They're high maintenance and they want way more than I do. I don't want any commitments, and I don't want anyone hanging around after I've gotten my rocks off. Jaded, I know, but I'm worn out. Tired of worrying if the condom busted, and tired of worrying if I even fucking remembered to put a rubber on! Casual fucks suck! Don't get me wrong, I'd love to someday have a meaningful relationship, you know, find my soul mate, but so far, no one has come close to getting me to that point.

Someone who actually wants to get to know *me* and likes me for what's in my heart, not how I look or what I do for a living. Olivia and I have talked about this a lot. She totally gets me and she pretty much called me a whore monger for what she called, 'dangerous, casual sex that will backfire on you'. She's a fucking mother for God's sake. She's got sons and she plays the devil's advocate so well.

One night, I got really drunk after the show. I went home by myself, minding my own business and these two chicks show up at my door. I'm pretty twisted off, so what the hell...I let them in. What happened after I closed the door has literally come back to haunt me and could end up costing me a lot of money by the time it's all said and done—not to mention hurt someone who means the world to me.

Brenna Martelli was one of the chicks, and her sidekick was a gal I only knew by the name of Red. You guessed it, she's got red-hair and a natural redhead at that. Yes siree, the carpet is the same color as the curtains, if ya know what I mean! Brenna and Red swing both ways so you can pretty much guess what happened that night. They put on quite a show for what seemed like hours. Watching those two go from taking tequila shots, to dancing with each other, to stripping, to taking turns getting each other off—a fucking wet dream in the flesh. Finally, Red motioned that it was my turn and I jumped on it like there was no tomorrow. Putting it to two at the same time? Yeah, crazy! Red got her phone and videoed the whole fuck fest. Who knew? And for the record, that saying, '*Hell hath no fury like a woman scorned*' is fucking true! I'm getting ahead of myself, so suffice it to say, we *will* revisit Brenna and Red later on in the story.

# BEST CUP OF COFFEE...
## EVER...

**WITH TOMMY SPENDING MORE AND MORE TIME WITH EMILY, YOURS TRULY,** Todd, took a back seat. It's all good, though—I mean, I'm really glad Tommy found someone. He deserves someone like Emily because he's good people and she's sheer perfection. The fact remains, though, that Tommy and I had spent so much time together that I really miss my best friend. More so than with the other guys in the band. We're all pretty tight, but Tommy—well, I told you about all that shit before.

I started getting back into my cars again, just to have something to occupy my spare time. The way I see it, you can never have enough tattoos or classic cars. I'm a vintage car collector, and I'll pay top dollar for the Mustangs. Those babies aren't cheap by any means, but worth every penny. Thank God my inheritance is hefty enough to support my habit. My all-time prize is a white '65 Shelby GT 350. She's got a 289-hp engine and can kick your ass on the highway. My grandpa bought it for me and we painstakingly restored it in his garage. She's my gal. I found another Shelby, in Evanston, that I now own and am in the process of restoring. Some professor from Northwestern was selling it and I just had to take a look. I was so excited that I got to Evanston two hours early, and he had a class so I went to a popular little coffee shop down by campus. By the looks of all the people waiting in line, it must be the main hangout of college students. I grabbed a newspaper, got my coffee, and sat down to read. Down time is good, right? The place was packed, and I was lucky to get the last table. Me and three empty chairs. The story of my life.

All of a sudden, I see this chick walking aimlessly around, holding her coffee, trying to talk on the phone, *and* manage a heavy backpack. Her coffee is spilling because she's got her hands full. She's looking around for a table but there isn't one. She's fucking –gorgeous–the prettiest thing I've ever seen and not like the typical dark haired, dark eyed skanky girls I usually lust after. This one's got blonde wavy hair down to her fine shapely ass. She's natural looking–hardly any makeup–and she's got these full, pink beautiful lips that make my dick rise to the occasion. I could see those lips all over my body. I shake my head and tell myself to just read my paper and mind my own business, but I can't. Something Olivia told me sticks in my head. In her own words, "When you meet your soul mate, you'll know it. Hands down it will flat ass slap you in the face. You'll know it, I promise." Well, I think I just found her. She glances over at my table with a contrite and shy look on her face. I look over the top of my RayBans, smile, and point my index finger to the empty chair across from me. She walks over to me.

"Are you sure?" she asks.

Trying to be über cool, I casually remark as I get up and pull the chair out, "Of course, please...sit." I immediately sit back down and think how dorky that remark was. I mean, I don't even know her and I'm fucking pulling the chair out for her? Geez!

Trying to play off that she's not affecting me, I glance down at my newspaper and pretend to be reading. She smiles and pulls out her books, placing them on the table and then gets out an arsenal of highlighters. "Thanks so much. I won't bother you, I promise," she says while smiling at me. She lays them out in some kind of ridiculous order, and while I'm *pretending* not to notice, I'm amused. She opens her backpack again, pulls out a book, and as she's reading, she highlights using the different colors. There is a definite method to her madness.

She suddenly notices me looking at her. "What?"

I quickly respond with my suave comeback, "Well, I was wondering if you brought a coloring book so we could both color." I say as I point to the highlighters. She sarcastically laughs, "Very funny."

I'm so into her, and I've got to get to know her. In my best pickup line,

I respond, "So, *very funny*, do you have a name?"

She rolls her eyes at me and cocks her pretty little head to the side, smiling, "Yes, Mr. RayBans, I do. It's Kyra."

"Kyra, it's nice to meet you, I'm Todd." I offer her my hand. She shakes it. I'm really pissing myself off with these fucking ridiculous social graces. Not in my character at all. *Get a grip, Todd, would you?*

She smiles pleasantly. "And, Todd, what brings you here? Are you a student at Northwestern?"

I throw my head back and laugh, "Pfft! Hell no!"

She nonchalantly picks up a highlighter and puts the end of it in her mouth. "So what brings you here among the masses of students then? Are you from here?"

I lean back in my chair and bite my bottom lip, trying to act cool. Seeing her put that fat highlighter in her mouth...Jesus that was sexy! *Be cool, dude.* "Nope. I live in Highland Park. I'm actually in Evanston to look at a classic car."

This piques her interest and she scoots her chair closer, while putting her elbows on the table. "Well, now you've got me curious...a classic car. Are you in the car business?"

I pull my sunglasses down and give her a cool little wink. "You've now exceeded your allotment of questions, Miss Kyra. I feel like we're playing charades and you've just spewed five in a row, in case you're not counting. And no, I'm not in the car business. I'm a musician, and I collect classic cars."

She looks turned off. "A musician, as in a band?"

"Affirmative."

"Well, does your band have a name?" she asks, flirtatiously.

"It does. It's called Avenue. Ever heard of it?"

She's definitely playing it cool. "Ummm, can't say as I have. What kind of music do you play?"

*Look at me, girl. What kind of music do you fucking think I play?*

We banter back and forth, and I get that she has a pre-conceived notion that guys who are in a band are all assholes. Point taken. We are. However, I'm willing to try and prove her wrong. We bullshit back and forth for about an hour and she breaks my heart when she says she has to leave to get to a class.

I pull my sunglasses off and set them on the table, smiling at her, and I give her another wink, "So, where does this leave us, beautiful?"

She laughs and shrugs her shoulders. "I have no idea. You tell me. Where *does* this leave us, Mr. Todd, the rock star? I've never met a guy in a band before, so I'm clueless. I'm not a groupie type and I haven't heard of your band, so I guess..."

I cut her off, pointing my finger at her laughing. "First off, saying you're not a groupie type was the *right* answer. Ding ding ding! You win! And I won't hold it against you because you haven't heard of my band."

She slings her gorgeous blonde hair over her shoulder then pulls it up in a knot and fucking sticks a pencil in it. A fucking pencil holding her hair up and she still looks beautiful. She chuckles, "Has anyone ever told you that you look like Ad..."

I hold my hand up and cut her off, "Adam Levine? Yeah. All the time. Why? Do you think he's hot?"

She shakes her head. "Well, *yeah!* Who doesn't?"

I tilt back in my chair, lace my fingers together, pop my knuckles and throw her a come on wink. "I believe you just paid me a compliment— either that or you're trying to come on to me."

She rolls her eyes before replying, "You are too much, Todd. Too much."

We exchange phone numbers, to which she replies sarcastically, "Well, Todd, it was nice meeting you. Thanks for sharing your table and I'll look forward to you calling. *NOT!*" She pulls her backpack over her shoulder and smiles in a flirty way. "I've heard how you band guys are, and I gotta get to class." And with that she's gone. I smile as she walks away and realize that I think I just met the mother of my children. My life just got better...fuckin-A!

I could tell she was surprised when I called her that night. "Hello?"

"Kyra?"

She's caught off guard. "Who is this?"

I laugh. "It's the hot rock star you met in the coffee shop today. You know, Adam Levine's twin."

She laughs, "I wasn't in a coffee shop today, sorry. Wrong person. Wrong number."

*Okay, baby cakes. I get it. You're playing hard to get, and I can play this game, too. You haven't seen my competitive side yet.*

We end up talking for two freakin' hours. I finally get the courage to ask if she wants to go out and she drops a bomb and breaks my heart. "Uhhh...thanks for the invite, but I'm really not into your scene. I'm just a plain old nerdy girl who goes to school and has no life to speak of. Thanks for calling, though. It was great meeting you, and I'll definitely look up your band."

Fuck me! I'm not taking no for an answer. "Wait! Kyra, you just broke my heart. Fucking broke my heart. Look, we can meet somewhere. Let's meet for coffee. Give me another chance and then decide if you want to go out with me or not. Coffee...no strings attached, just coffee. Come on, Kyra. What do ya say?"

She laughs. "Okay. I guess we could meet for coffee. I'd like that."

We meet up for coffee the day after next. I swear to God, Olivia was right. This girl *is* the one for me. When she walks into our coffee shop—I call it 'our coffee shop' because that's where we met—she has her hands behind her back and walks up to me, grinning from ear to ear. "What's up with the smile?" I ask.

She proudly places a black t-shirt on the table. "Here, I got this for you. It's corny, I know."

I unfold the shirt and read it. I smile and take her hand. The shirt says, 'Plays Well With Others'. "Wow. This is awesome, Kyra. I love it!"

She makes a silly face, "Well, I know you play in a band, and I thought it was cool. Corny but cool. So you really do like it?"

I give her a hug, and when she hugs me back, I'm relieved. "It's awesome, Kyra. I really do love it."

She pulls back. "Seriously? I was afraid you'd laugh at me."

I put her hair behind her ear and look her in the eye. "I'd never laugh at you, Kyra. I really love it. I'm gonna wear it every day."

We both laugh, and I badger her to go out on a date. She won't commit. I swear to God I've never had to beg for a girl to go out with me, and I have a feeling I'm gonna have to with her.

Since our 'coffee date', we talk on the phone every day. What the fuck? I can't believe I'm so nervous about asking her out. Afraid she'd say no I guess. I finally get up enough courage. "So, beautiful, what do you say we take this up a notch, say from a coffee shop to a restaurant?"

"Are you asking me out on a date?" she jokingly asks.

I laugh to myself. *Yes, Kyra, whatever your last name is, I'm asking you out on a date. Note to self...ask her last name, dickhead!*

"Yeah. I guess you could say I'm asking you out on an official date. Where would you like to go, Miss Kyra? I'll take you anywhere you wanna go."

"Surprise me."

"I can certainly do that, but you may be sorry...Oh, by the way, do you have a last name?"

She giggles into the phone, "I do. It's Edwards."

"Well, goodnight, Kyra Edwards. I will pick you up tomorrow night at seven. And by the way, before you have to ask me, my last name is O'Malley."

"I know that already. I looked you up on the internet."

I can't resist, "Well, if it's on the internet, it must be true. See you tomorrow night, Kyra Edwards. Sleep tight, beautiful."

# A Real Date...

**I'VE BEEN A FUCKING NERVOUS WRECK ALL DAY. DATE NIGHT IS HERE. THE** guys even noticed it. I was the brunt of their jokes because I'd mentioned I met a girl, and of course they couldn't wait to be asswipes. We practiced for a while, but I wasn't into it.

I really want to impress Kyra, so I pull out the nice clothes. Nice to me is a black button down shirt, kinda wrinkled, and a pair of clean jeans with my high-top Chucks. Normally, I'm all about the torn jeans and t-shirts, but tonight I need to impress a beautiful lady. I look in the mirror, fuck with my hair, marvel at myself, give myself a pep talk that she's gonna love me, take a deep breath, and I'm out the door to pick up my date.

I get to her apartment building and immediately realize this chick lives a life of privilege. The building is on Lake Shore Drive, kinda close to Mr. H's condo. Nice digs. Very nice. Fuckin-A! *Maybe I should have brought her flowers. No, that's stupid. Shit!* I ring the bell, and she buzzes me in. I stand at the intercom as she says, "Hi. I'm on the sixth floor. Number 669," Okay...I got the sixty nine and I laugh as I ride the elevator up. I casually knock. She answers the door, and it's all I can do to keep from picking her ass up and taking her into the nearest bedroom and proceed to fuck her lights out. Here I am, dressed up trying to impress her, and she's fucking wearing jeans with holes in them and a skimpy tank top that makes me horny as hell.

We stand there looking at each other. I shrug my shoulders. Finally, she starts to laugh so hard she has to hold her side. I look at her, "What's so damn funny?"

She catches her breath. "Oh my God! I can't believe it. I tried to impress you and show you I could dress like a girl going out with a rock star and you show up dressed like..."

Now I'm pissed. I fucking dressed up for this chick and she's making fun of me? *Oh fuck no!*

I take a deep breath and suck it up. She can tell I'm not cool with her joking around and puts her hand over her mouth to muffle the sound. "Look, Todd, I'm sorry. I just meant that I was trying to impress *you*." She looks down at the floor, puts her hand on her forehead, and shakes her head. "I knew this wasn't gonna turn out good. I totally suck at this."

I realize that I overreacted. I'm on the defensive, and I'm not used to this. Chicks don't crack up when they see me, they *worship* me! I need to switch gears, and fast, or this is going in the toilet. I take a deep breath and take her into my arms. "Babe, you don't suck at anything. I was just kicking myself in the ass because I tried to impress *you*. Look, I don't dress like this for just anyone, ya know. You're the classiest chick I've ever been with...well not *been* with, but taken out on a date, and I'm just as nervous as you." I brush her hair behind her ear. "If you wanna change, I can just make myself a drink or something... or I can go home and change and come back. Your choice."

Looking relieved, she smiles and bites her bottom lip. "There's beer in the fridge. I won't be long."

Long is an understatement. I grab a beer and take a walk around her place. It's contemporary with grey walls, white furniture, and a huge white shaggy rug. I think to myself how I'd love to lay on that thing with her, butt ass naked and shagging *her*. A huge state of the art TV graces the wall above the fireplace. I flip the remote on and 'The Voice' comes on. Fucking Adam Levine is turning his chair around. Kyra walks out and her eyes light up when she sees the TV and points. "See, I *told* you that you look like him, didn't I?"

I shake my head. "Yeah, you did. You look great, by the way." I grab the remote, aim it at the TV, turn it off, and wink at her. "Fuck Adam

Levine, let's go out on our date. Adam has his red chair and I've got you tonight."

"You look really nice, Todd. And I really wasn't laughing at you. I was more laughing at me. I'm such a dork."

I think to myself, *No. You're the most beautiful girl in the world.*

We grab a nice dinner at Magnolia Cafe. She's *definitely* not shy about ordering food, which is cool with me. I laugh as she orders not only one, but *two* appetizers. I love to eat, and I love a girl who is secure enough to just fucking order what she wants and not pretend she doesn't eat. Hesitantly, she puts her fingers up to those gorgeous lips and looks at me. "Is that okay? You'll share with me, won't you?"

"Hell yeah, beautiful. Knock yourself out! We can share, for sure."

She scrunches her face; she's so damn cute. "Sorry, but I'm starved."

So, that's one more thing I like about Kyra Edwards. She eats.

After dinner, I take her to a little jazz bar on Broadway called the Green Mill Cocktail Lounge. We walk in and grab a table. "Ever been here?" I ask.

She shakes her head no and I'm not sure of her take on it, so I start spouting trivia about the place. "Green Mill's been here since 1907. See that booth over there?" I point and she nods. "That was Al Capone's personal booth back in the day."

She's shocked. "Really?"

"Yep. He liked it because it had a clear view to the front and back doors for easy exit. You know how those gangstas are." I point to the stage, "And up there, on certain nights, they do slam poetry if you're into that. I'm not a fan, but if you are, we could..."

She nods. "I've never watched it, but one of the girls in my study group raves about it."

*Note to self: I think that means she'd like to come back on slam poetry night.*

So, our first 'date' is going awesome. I know you wanna ask me how I'm feeling, so I'll tell you I'm feeling abso-fucking-lutely pumped and this chick is off the charts a TEN. I feel so at ease talking to her. Intelligent conversation and she doesn't judge me or expect me to be anything other than what I am. I take her hand across the table and look at her. I smile because it makes her uncomfortable. She starts nervously twirling her hair.

"What? What are you staring at?" she asks.

"You, babe. I'm staring at you." I lean across the table and look her square in the eye. "You're fucking gorgeous. Has anyone ever told you that?"

She slings her hair back over her shoulder and laughs. "No one has ever said I was *effing* gorgeous, Todd. You're the first."

She looks like she's having a good time. I can tell by her body language. The band takes a break and music comes on. It's one of my all-time favorites by The Ramones, "I Wanna be Sedated." As soon as I hear it, I grab her hand. "Oh, hell yeah, we're dancing to this!" She's a freaking awesome dancer, and we dance until our sides hurt.

I'm careful not to overindulge in alcohol, and she's drinking mineral water. The music tonight is awesome, so we scoot our chairs around to face the stage, and I casually put my arm around her. She's cool with it and I'm relieved. I don't know why I'm so cautious. I just don't want to fuck this up.

Our date ends with me walking her into her building. I'm hoping like hell she asks me up, but fuck no...it ain't happening.

We stop by the elevator and she gets her keys out. "Thanks so much for an amazing date, Todd. I had a really good time."

I look at her and realize she's fucking serious. Date over? See ya?

I get my nerve up. "So, do you wanna go out again?"

She smiles this huge smile. "Sure. I'd like that."

What the hell, here goes. I pull her closer to me. She lets out this cute little gasping noise and moans when I kiss her. FUCKING moans into my mouth. I *feel* it, too, and I've got a hard on like no tomorrow. I'm about to explode. I kiss her with all I have. Her lips are the absolute softest I've ever felt and my tongue is savoring every inch of her mouth. I've fucking never, ever, in my life felt this way when I kissed a girl. I put my hands on her face and kiss every inch of it. All I can think about is the next time I'll see her. She puts her fingers on my mouth and traces my lips as she looks at my face and whispers, "You're..."

I take her fingers and kiss them as I laugh, "Spending the night, right?" I joke.

She rolls her eyes and shakes her head, "In your dreams, Todd. In your dreams. I was gonna say that you're a really, really good kisser."

I pout. "So, this was really a good night and you're saying I *can't* spend the night?"

She nods yes. "It was a really fun night. And no, you're definitely NOT spending the night. I've got a test to study for and you've probably got fan girls waiting at your house."

I talk her into letting me ride up the elevator with her and at least seeing her inside safely, thinking she may change her mind. Nada. I turn to walk away and she calls out to me.

"Todd?"

I turn around thinking she's had a change of heart. "Yeah?"

"Goodnight," she whispers.

I smile and blow her a kiss. "Goodnight, Kyra Edwards. I'll see ya real soon."

I can't get her out of my mind. I want to tell someone about her so bad, so I call Olivia. The fucking call goes to her voicemail and I'm pissed. She *always* answers when I call her. FUCK! Olivia and I share everything, and right now, I really need to talk to her. I laugh to myself and shake my head. Olivia is old enough to be my mother, but I can talk to her about anything, and I mean *anything*. I've told her shit I haven't told anyone, and I'm not ashamed or embarrassed. She's not, either. Hell, she even knows about my Prince Albert piercing.

I leave her a voicemail, "Hey, where are you? I really need to talk to you. Can you call me, por favor? Doesn't matter how late, just call me." And I quickly follow up with a text. No response. Damn. She and Mr. H must be 'busy'.

# THE THING THAT WOULDN'T LEAVE

**I GET HOME AND THERE'S A CAR IN MY DRIVEWAY. THE MOTOR IS RUNNING** and it's blocking me from getting in the garage. I lay on the horn because I'm not expecting anyone. The car door opens and Brenna gets out. Fuckin-A. Not what I need right now. I step out of my car and she walks up, putting her arm around me. I remove her arm, "Hey, Brenna. It's kinda late. What's up?"

She looks at me, seductively licking her lips and moving her body into mine, which is a turn off. "I just thought we could hang out. I'm actually kinda horny."

Jesus H Christ. What did I do to deserve this? Wait, I know. I fucked her and her friend at the same time, that's what I did. I quickly try to diffuse the situation. "Look, Brenna, I'm just back from rehearsal and I've gotta get some shut eye. I'm fucking beat and I can't get my pinkie up, much less my dick."

She follows me to the door, not taking no for an answer. "I'll just stay the night and we'll see what comes up in the morning." She pinches my ass and I cringe.

Arghh... Okay. I'm gonna tell her. "Brenna, look...this isn't gonna work out between me and you. We had fun, but I'm actually seeing someone." I turn to walk in my house and she grabs my arm, looking at me with hate in her eyes. This chick is fixing to go postal.

She screams at me and I just hope the neighbors don't hear. "Wait, did you just say you're *seeing* someone? Are you fucking kidding me?" She kicks my door. "Oh *hell* no! I'm not taking a second seat, mother fucker! Who is she?" She's pointing her finger at me, and I realize she's a total nut case.

I pull out my phone and get in her face. "Look, bitch—you want me to call the cops? Ya wanna go to jail? Because you *will* if you don't get your crazy ass off my property NOW! You're nothing to me! Got it? Nothing! I fucked you and your fuck buddy...that's it. Now get in your car and fucking leave!"

I push her backwards all the way to her car and she gets in, shaking her finger at me. "You're gonna regret this!" She screams at me. I flip her off. "You think I'm scared of you? Bring it, bitch!" I back my car into the street and watch as she backs out, her tires squealing and she's gone.

Walking in the front door, I flip the locks and fling my keys inside. I'm so goddamn mad right now I'm shaking. My phone rings, and thinking it's Brenna, I answer, "Bitch, what didn't you get about '*fucking leave*'?" There's a brief silence.

"Todd?" this soft, sweet voice says. My heart sinks as I realize its Kyra.

"Hey...what's up, babe?"

Click. She hangs up. Hell, I would have, too. *Jesus Christ. What have I done?*

I dial her number and it goes straight to voicemail. I throw my head back in frustration and kick the door. Fuck it. I don't need this. I haven't done anything wrong, well, in the last three weeks anyway. I throw my phone against the wall and it shatters. *Cool move, Todd. That just cost you about four hundred dollars, asshole!*

Grabbing a beer from the fridge, I pop the top, look at the can, and toss it into the trash. I need fucking hard alcohol, so I grab a bottle of scotch and head for my room. Stripping naked, I hop into my bed under the cool sheets and start with a swig, then another and another until I pass out.

I wake with a nasty, dry taste in my mouth, and I squint as I see the sunlight peeking in through the blinds. My head is throbbing. I get up, look outside, and there, parked in my driveway is Brenna.

I throw on some boxers and walk over the gravel driveway barefoot.

She's asleep in her car and I pound on the window, startling her awake. I point to the street, "You.Need.To.Leave.Now!" I'm really pissed when she just looks at me. I can tell she's been crying, and I don't want anything to do with this head case.

She rolls the window down and I look inside. "Brenna, look... I told you last night that I'm seeing someone. I'd really like you to leave."

She starts her car and backs out of the driveway, flipping me off as she drives away. I go back into the house, and my first thought is to call Kyra, but my fucking phone is in pieces on the kitchen floor.

I throw on some jeans and the t-shirt she gave me and decide to head over to her place. I ring the buzzer and no one answers, so I decide to sit in the lobby and wait. Finally, I see her walk in. Her hair is pulled back in a ponytail, and she's got black running shorts and a hot pink top on. She's out of breath and it looks like she's been running. She bends down, puts her hands on her knees and stares at me. "What are you doing here, Todd?"

I try and explain what happened last night, and she's definitely not buying it. "Look, it's not a big deal. We just went out on one date. We're not in a relationship or anything, so I really have no reason to be mad." She takes a swig from her water bottle. "I think we should just say we had a nice date and end it there. I told you that I'm not in the groupie league, and I don't need that in my life, so I guess I'll see you around."

She walks towards the elevator and I follow her. "Look, Kyra, I can explain. It's really not a big deal. I had a one nighter with this chick before I met you, and she thought it was more than it was. It's as simple as that."

She's biting her lip. "Look, I told you, I'm not into all that stuff. You're who you are—a rock star—and I'm a student. Can't you see? We have nothing in common."

Fucking-A. Why does my life have to be so complicated? Why do all the people I care about just leave me? First my parents, then my Grammy, and now Kyra?

The elevator dings and she turns to me. "For what it's worth, I *did* try to call you back but it rang and rang. Then went to voicemail. You must have been busy." She looks at me with a shit eating grin, "Nice t-shirt, by the way." I hold the elevator doors open. "Look, Kyra, I threw my phone last night and it broke. I don't have a phone right now."

She winks and pushes the button to her floor. "Maybe you should get a new one."

# A SECOND DATE?

WITH MY NEW PHONE, I DIAL HER NUMBER AND SHE ANSWERS. "ARE YOU stalking me?"

I laugh. "Yeah, I guess I am. Ya wanna try this again?"

"Try what?"

"Try...anything. Can I take you to dinner?"

She agrees to dinner and I'm pumped. I call Olivia and Mr. H answers her phone.

"What's up, man? Can I talk to Olivia?"

He tells me that her gallbladder burst and that she's in the hospital. Jesus! Not what I expected to hear, so I jump in my car, and I'm freaking out on my way to the hospital. *Please don't tell me that someone else I care about is leaving me. Fuck! What have I done to deserve this?*

I get to the hospital in record time, and I smile when I open the door to her room and see her lying there with tubes hooked up to her. She's my fucking best friend and she gets me. She looks really tired but makes me come sit on the bed beside her. I kiss her cheek, take her hand, and I tell her I've met a girl. Her face lights up and she makes me tell her all about meeting Kyra. She laughs when she reads the t-shirt Kyra bought me.

Mr. H is sitting on the couch, working, and won't let me stay long, but at least I get to see her. She's gonna be okay, and that's all I care about. She could have died if she didn't get to the hospital when she did.

They said her damn gallbladder was about to burst. Mr. H told me she was being hard headed about going to the emergency room which doesn't surprise me in the least. She's one stubborn woman—there's no doubt.

When I think about the possibility of losing someone else who means the world to me, I get scared. I've lost too many of the people I love. I say my goodnights to Olivia and she points her finger at me telling me to be on my best behavior when I take Kyra on our date. She reminds me to dress nice. Jesus! I swear that must be a girl thing because guys couldn't give a shit what you wear when ya go out. I promise her I'll represent well.

After much thought, I decide to take Kyra to a nice fancy restaurant— some place where you dress nice and use your good manners, like Olivia suggested. That should impress her. I need to let her know that I'm serious about getting to know her better and that I'm a good guy.

I go to pick her up, and when she answers the door, I smell food. She smiles and bites her bottom lip, which in itself is a fucking turn on. "I decided to cook, and I rented us some movies. I hope you don't mind." She has an uncertain look on her face.

*Do I mind? Hell to the no! I'm in heaven.*

She's made us some kind of fancy pasta and this huge bowl of salad. I grab two wine glasses from the rack, a bottle of wine from the fridge, and help her in the kitchen as she sets our places on the bar. She nods with her head toward the refrigerator. "There's beer if you'd rather have that. I hope you like pasta. That's about all I can cook."

I open the wine bottle. "No beer. Wine is great. Let's toast."

She laughs as she takes her glass. "Toast to...?"

"You and me, baby. Let's toast to us."

After dinner, we go to the living room, and she's got *The Notebook* cued up to watch. She giggles. "It's a chick flick. You haven't seen it, have you?"

I shake my head no and scrunch my face reluctantly. "Ehhh, okay whatever. I'll try anything once."

Hell, I'll watch *anything* with her.

I motion to her and she scoots over by me on the couch as I move her into my arms. She doesn't resist. About halfway into the movie, which isn't too bad I might add, I kiss her and she responds. She does that little gasp and moan and I laugh. "I love when you do that."

She turns around. "Do what?"

"Moan into my mouth, babe. When I kiss you, you make this cute little noise that drives me wild."

She puts her head on my shoulder. "You're a good kisser."

"Yeah?"

She moans, "Ummm...yeah."

I'm not sure how to handle this. I wanna do things right, but shit! What do I do? She's waiting for me to make the first move.

I start to unbutton her shirt and she doesn't stop me. I've gotten to the last button, and goddamn, she's got a sexy light pink bra on. Sliding my hand inside, I play with her nipples and she does that little moaning thing again. Something about this whole night is lyrical. I make a move. She responds. It's like a play of emotions, and she's not like any girl I've ever been with. Other girls would have already had their clothes off pulling my dick out of my pants to suck it, only to jump on it and ride. But this...It's so different.

It's almost like the first time you feel a girl up in middle school. Your dick is throbbing in your pants and you can feel the explosion about to happen. I reach around and find a way to get her bra unhooked and her breasts are exposed. They are the most beautiful little things I've ever seen. Tiny, dark nipples standing at attention from my touch are pretty good indicators she's turned on.

I put her hand on my crotch so she can feel me. She's breathing heavily as she unbuttons my jeans. I kick them off and spring free. She touches my dick, which sends me over the edge. "Holy fuck!" I gasp. At my reaction, she quickly moves her hand like she's embarrassed, like she's touched a forbidden fruit. I take her hand in mine and kiss it. "Baby, I want you so bad. Touch me."

She puts her hand back and I help her. We have this incredible make-out fest, and I'm dying to get inside her. I feel like she's unsure about this and I've got an idea. I've got to see her fully naked body and I want her to feel like this is about just me and her.

"Where's the bathroom?" I whisper in her ear.

"Second door on the right, why?" She points as she's panting with want.

I sit up and turn her to face me. "Trust me." I wink as I take her hand

and pull her up from the couch, leading us into the bathroom. I unbutton her jeans and pull them down while I'm kissing her and she steps out of them. I lift her up and place her on the vanity as I turn on the shower. She's looking at me and, cautiously, she asks, "What are you doing?"

I put my finger over my lips. "Shh...You got any candles?" She nods and points back into the living room. I kiss her hands and put them together in her lap. "Hold that thought," I say and come back with a few, and we light them together. I switch the lights off and she smiles.

"This is nice. It's like something from a movie. I had no idea you were a romantic."

I straddle her and lightly push her back against the mirror, kissing her. "This is gonna be an academy award winner, just wait. And for the record, I'm a hopeless romantic."

I extend my hand and she hops off the vanity as I stare at her beautiful body. She tries to cover herself with her hands, but I remove them. I quickly pull my shirt off and stand there looking at this picture of perfection. Her skin is pale white and so soft. I can't stop looking at her naked body and I feel like she's uncomfortable because she grabs a towel and wraps it around her. I undo the towel and let it fall to the floor. "Will you stop with the covering up your body? Why do you do that?"

She stands there with her hands at her side, looking into my eyes with almost innocent anticipation. I scratch my eyebrow with my thumb and shake my head. I put my hands on her shoulders and reassure her. "Kyra...goddamn, woman...your body is fucking beautiful. Let me show you how beautiful you are to me." I guide her into the shower and she sits on the seat inside, crossing her legs. It's so damn cute. I have to laugh at how inhibited she is. She bites the corner of her lip and exhales. Her foot is nervously shaking and I grin. "Ya ready for a little fun?"

I look around and see all kinds of girly liquid soaps on the shower shelf so I grab a random bottle, smell it, and she laughs. "Does it meet your expectations?"

"Oh, baby, you have no idea. Is this shampoo?" She nods as I squirt some of it into my hand and start by massaging it into her scalp. There's that cute little moan again. "Oh, this is nice."

"Yeah?" I whisper as I nip at her ear.

"Oh yes...*Very* nice." She smiles with closed eyes and leans her head back.

I put some soap on my hands and start to wash her. She reciprocates by squirting soap on her hands and rubs it onto my body. Her touch and the slick sensation of the soap makes me realize I need to slow down or I'm gonna blow before I even get inside her. I rinse her hair and slowly run my fingers through the long strands. She opens her eyes and looks down at my piercing. She has a curious and kind of scared look on her face.

I reassure her, "It's called a Prince Albert, baby, and I can rock your world with it." I tap her nose and I'm surprised at her reaction.

She looks even more freaked out.

I take her face into my hands. "What's wrong, baby? It won't hurt you. It's a pleasure tool."

"Ummm...Okay," she reluctantly says.

Her body language tells me she's not cool with it.

I kiss her face. "I *can* take it out. Do you want me to?"

She's embarrassed as she puts her face into my chest. "Please. You don't mind, do you?"

I tilt her head up and look into those gorgeous blue eyes. "Of course I don't mind, silly." I reach down and quickly remove it, placing the metal u-shaped ring on the shower shelf. "Here. Look it's out." She looks down, then over on the shelf, and I see her crack a smile.

"It doesn't bite, though. I promise."

We stand under the warmth of the shower, and I hold her close to me. My heart is beating fast, and she giggles, which makes me grin. I tip her chin up with my finger. "What's so funny?"

"Your heart is beating really fast," she softly says.

"Fuckin-A it is. You're killing me. Let's get out, we're pruning."

I lift her and carry her to the bed, and I can't wait to get inside her.

Immediately, she pulls the covers over her and tenses up. "What's wrong, babe?"

She closes her eyes and scrunches her face. "I'm not on birth control."

I look into that beautiful face and kiss her nose. "I've gotcha covered—or should I say, I've got *it* covered. Be right back."

I hop out of bed, run into the living room, and grab a condom from my wallet. I rip the pack open with my teeth and slap that sucker on in record time. She's sitting up in bed, waiting for me, and smiles when I climb back into bed.

I breathe in through my teeth. "I've waited for this moment since the day I met you, I hope you know. Now, where were we?" I part her legs with mine and seductively rock as I start to enter her. As I push in, she flinches. She's tight. Way too tight. Her body tenses and her hands grab my arms as she pleads, "Please...Be gentle."

*Fuck...Is she still a virgin?* Surely not. When you're in this situation and your balls are bursting, what do you do? I need some help here. Should I ask her? Okay, here goes.

I pull out and take her face into my hands. "Kyra, are you a...a virgin?"

She gasps, "Yes, but don't stop. Please."

"Baby, look, let's stop this before we start. I'm not doing this. I can't take your virginity."

I try to get up and she pulls me back down. "I want this."

"You should have told me."

She reaches down, takes my dick with her hand and guides it inside her. "Look, I said I want this. Don't you want me?"

I gasp. "Fuck woman I want you more than roses need the rain!"

"Then do it." She begs.

She's wet as I push slow and try to go easy. She moves her hips up, which is driving me wild. She grabs my ass, and I push harder as she accepts me. She closes her eyes and whimpers.

"You okay, baby?" God she's so tight, and I don't want to hurt her.

I'm pissed that she didn't tell me, but I can't stop. I feel myself push into her and break what she's kept for so long. She lets out a deep breath and the reality hits me. I really *am* her first.

I feel her body stiffen, and she's holding on to me so tight. Her nails are digging into my arms as she screams out my name, and that's all I need before I blow my load. I feel her body quiver as I move off of her and turn on the light and see her face. "Baby, why didn't you tell me?"

She's embarrassed and moves across me to switch off the light. I put my hand on hers. "Don't."

I take her hair and brush it back from her face. "Why, baby?"

"Why what?" she defensively asks.

"Why didn't you tell me you were a virgin?"

She puts her forearm over her face. "Does it matter?"

I remove her arm and stroke her face. "Yes, of course it matters. You should have told me."

She turns on her side away from me, and I turn her over to face me. "Kyra, babe. Look, I'm so sorry. I should have stopped."

She has tears in her eyes and looks at me with anger on her face. "Pfft. Great. Just great. Thanks. That's just what I always envision the first man I have sex with to say to me. 'I'm so sorry.' Perfect."

She starts to cry. I try to talk to her and she shakes her head and turns away from me. She won't talk. I get out of the bed, take the condom off, throw it in the trash, and slam my fist into the wall. "Fuck it!" She sits up in the bed and holds her pillow to her stomach. Her body is shaking and she starts to cry uncontrollably. She looks at me like she wants me to say something, and I don't know what to say. It seems like I'm the biggest fuck up and no matter how I try, I just keep screwing things up. I didn't mean for my words to come out like that, and she took it wrong. No, take that back, I *said* them all wrong. Fuck, I just need to get the hell out of here and think things through. I'm not used to having to defend my words, and I flat ass fucked up.

I get back in bed and turn her on her side, rocking her in my arms and kissing her head. I can feel her body shake as she eventually cries herself to sleep. I can't sleep. What the fuck have I just done? I have nothing to offer her, I've just taken her virginity, *and* I'm scum of the earth. I lay with her in my arms and watch her sleep.

She's the most beautiful girl I've ever seen, and she's curled up with her hand under her cheek, peacefully sleeping. All I can think of is I need to get the hell out of here and get out of her life before I cause her more pain.

I carefully slide out of bed, throw on my clothes, and bail. I take the easy way out. I stop in the kitchen and think that maybe I should leave a note. I can't. What the hell would I even say? I pass through the living room see the TV still on, displaying a blank screen. I turn it off, leave a lamp on, and I'm outta here. All the way home I think what a fuck up I am. I'm a piece of shit, and I don't deserve her. I pull into my driveway, go into the house, pull out the bottle of scotch, and drink until I pass out. I hate myself right about now.

# Repercussions and Redemption

**The next day, I wake up still hating myself. I've found someone I** care about, and I don't think there is any damage control I can do to fix this.

I miss rehearsal, and the guys are calling me nonstop. It's not like me to miss a rehearsal. Hell, I'm the one who always says there's no excuse to miss a rehearsal. I get a text from Tommy. *'What's up?'*

I text back, *'Nothin. Layin low for a while.'*

For three days I stay locked up in my house. I don't want to be around anyone. I'm thinking over my life, the people who have come and gone, the person I am, the man I want to be, and how I've totally fucked everything up. I've hurt someone I care deeply about and I'm not even man enough to face her and admit it. I took the chicken shit way out and I pretty much hate myself right now. I've finally found a girl I think is the one; she's smart, she's as beautiful on the inside as she is on the outside, and I want to be with her so damn bad. I replay that night in my head over and over and I think of what I should have done differently. Her virginity can't be taken back, and my actions can't, either.

Olivia is the one person I can talk to, so I call her, and she can tell by the sound of my voice that something's wrong. She tells me to come over. I get to her house, and when she answers the door, she has her arms open and gives me the hug I so badly need. Once I tell her what's gone down, I knew she wouldn't let me off the hook and she pretty much tells me what I knew she would. She makes me call Kyra. "Think of what she's going through. She gave you her body and soul and you just left her. That's not the Todd I know. You need to call her, but you really should have called her three days ago."

She makes me go upstairs, and I nervously dial Kyra's number. Maybe she won't answer. She answers on the third ring. "What, Todd? Why are you calling me?"

"Babe, we need to talk."

She's crying and it breaks my heart. Then she gets angry. "Don't you dare call me *babe,* and just exactly what do you think we need to talk about? I mean, correct me if I'm wrong, Todd, but you were the one who left and obviously didn't want to talk that night. So what's changed?"

"I need you, babe."

She laughs sarcastically. "Yeah, right. You need me. Good one. I should have known better, though. You band guys are all alike. Love 'em and leave 'em. I'm just another statistic you can add to your collection of conquests."

"No, Ky, that couldn't be farther from the truth. Please. Can I come over? Can we just talk? I'm dyin' here. Look, I know I've hurt you. I'm hurting, too. Just please let me come over. Please?"

She reluctantly agrees, and before I know it, I'm in my car and on my way over to her place. She buzzes me in, and I stand at her door a broken man. I look at her face, see the hurt, and realize she's a broken woman.

I hand her flowers and a bottle of wine Olivia sent with me, and she takes them cautiously as I walk in. "These are for you. A peace offering, a fresh start." I explain.

We talk in the living room and she pretty much opens up and tells me what a scum bag I am.

The conversation goes from talking, to her screaming at me. As she's yelling, everything she's saying is the truth. I take her into my arms. "Kyra, I've been miserable since I left you. Never, ever in my life have I felt the feelings I have for you. I screwed up. I want you in my life, babe. Let me make it up to you."

She breaks my hold, "Make it up to me? Seriously? How do you propose to do that, Todd?" She waves her hands through the air. "Wait, do I even really want you to make anything up to me? You're an asshole. I think I hate you. Do you even know what I've been going through?"

I pull her back into me, "I *do* know what you've been going through, Kyra. Goddammit! Don't hate me. I bailed because I...I was scared. You were a virgin, and I took that from you. I have nothing to offer you, Kyra. I'm a musician, I'm fixing to go out on the road for months and you're... you're so smart and you have such a promising life ahead of you. You don't need someone like me."

She breaks my hold on her, "And you think that by screwing me and leaving that you've done me right? I didn't even deserve you staying the night and saying it was over to my face? A note? An 'it was great' or 'it really sucked'?"

I hang my head and take her hands in mine. "Kyra, it didn't suck. It was amazing, and it was making love, not screwing. To top that, I don't think it's over—at least I hope it's not." I take her face in my hands and wipe her tears with my thumb. "I think it's just begun." I slowly back her up to the wall and raise her hands above her head. She's staring me in the eye, and I know she's still mad and hurt.

"Kyra, I know you're gonna think this is bullshit, but you're what I've been looking for my whole life. Look, I fucked up. I know it, but just hear me out. Let's work through this."

We talk for hours, and I tell her everything about me; things I've never told anyone. I've never been one to express my real feelings. I'm not used to having to sell someone on me, but I'm determined to let her know I don't want things to end with us.

"Kyra, I care about you, more than you know. There was a reason you sat at my table that day in the coffee shop. It was fate."

She cocks her head back. "Really? Because I'm still having a hard time with it, Todd. Three days—*three days*—and you didn't even call. I can't forget that."

She's shaking her head and sobbing, and it breaks my heart. "You waited 'til I was asleep and just left. I felt like one of those groupies you talk about. Some girl you're ashamed of, I...I can't..."

I take her hands, angry that she'd even think that. "Shhh...I'm not ashamed of you, and you're not a fucking groupie. Don't ever say that, Kyra." I tip her face up to mine. "You're my special angel." She cries harder and I pick her up and carry her into the bedroom. Placing her in bed, I wrap her in my arms. We're fully clothed and I rock her. The feel of her in my arms somehow makes me feel complete. Just before I fall asleep, I whisper in her ear, "I'm not leaving. I need you, babe. We can stay up and talk longer if you want. You can call me out all night. I deserve it. I'll take it like a man."

"I'm emotionally spent; these past few days have worn me down. Besides, I have an early class tomorrow. I have to go because I haven't been there all week. Right now, I just want to go to sleep," she whispers back.

"And by the way, I'm not having sex with you." She slaps my arm.

I laugh and kiss the top of her head, "No sex, baby. This isn't about sex. Just let me hold you."

"I still think I hate you," she whispers.

"That's okay, but I think I'm falling in love with you, Kyra." I pull her closer into me,

"You have no idea what you do to me."

Her radio is on, oldies are playing—Carole King is singing "Will You Still Love Me Tomorrow". She sits up when she hears it, "Oh my GAWD!" She turns on the light and runs the back of her hand across her nose then wipes the tears from her eyes with both hands and quickly moves over me to turn it off.

I grab her hand, "Don't. I like that song." I turn her over to face me and sing the song to her. With my finger, I softly trace hearts on her face and I look into her eyes. Tears fall from them as I kiss her eyes. "Don't cry, baby."

"What are you doing?" she asks.

"I'm kissing your tears away. No more tears. We're moving forward—past this. Give me your heart, Kyra." I trace little hearts on her chest.

She looks at me and puts two fingers on my lips. "Can I ask you something?"

"Of course you can." I put my hand over her fingers.

"Have you been with a lot of virgins?"

I smile. "Do you want to know the truth?"

She shrugs her shoulders. "I don't know. Do I?"

"No, baby, I haven't, but I can tell you that me being your first was the absolute best feeling in the world. Do you have any clue how amazing that was?"

"Really?" she whispers.

I pull her to me and breathe into her hair, "Seriously really. Now, can I ask you something?"

"Yes. What do you want to know?"

"Baby, why did you wait so long to have sex? You don't have to tell me, I just wondered."

She closes her eyes and puts her hands over her face. I pull her hands down.

"I just never found anyone who made me *feel* before. I didn't want to have sex just to be doing it, and I wanted to wait for the right guy... Someone who made my body ache with desire. God, that sounded really corny didn't it?" She puts her hands back over her face.

"Not at all. So I made you ache with desire?"

She nods her head and laughs. "No, you hurt the crap out of me!"

I'm shocked. "I did? You mean it didn't feel good?"

"It did feel good. It just hurt at first."

"So about the aching with desire thingy. Did I do that to you?"

She giggles. "Yes, you did, but don't go getting the big head."

"Too late. I already have the big head. I got it the night I made love to you. Let's get some shut eye. You have class tomorrow."

The next morning, she wakes up to find me propped up on an elbow staring at her. I woke really early and it was so peaceful just watching her sleep. Her hand was tucked under her chin and she was curled up almost in a fetal position. She's beautiful—the most beautiful thing I've ever seen. She wakes, sees me and yawns. Then she stretches.

I pinch her side and tease. "Hey, you. I'm still here, see?"

She laughs. "I see that."

I move to kiss her and she stops me. "Nooooo. I have morning breath!"

"I don't care."

She raises up, looks over at the wall and points. "Well, I do and besides, there's still a hole in my wall."

I give her my most pitiful look ."So, no kiss and I'm still in the doghouse until I get it fixed?"

She rolls over on top of me, and messes up my hair. "Yup. Still in the doghouse, you dawg!"

"Ummmm...do I smell coffee?" she anxiously asks.

I bring her a cup and follow her into the bathroom while she gets dressed for class.

I hop up on the vanity, grinning and watching as she showers then gets dressed. She looks at me and laughs because my hair is really messed up. She shakes her head, rolls her eyes and turns me to face the mirror while she fixes my hair with her fingers then stands back satisfied. "There, you look better now."

"See, I do need you, Ky."

"No one's ever called me Ky,"

I laugh. "So I'm your first lay *and* the first to call you Ky?"

She slaps my arm and gives me a pouty look.

"I wrote a song for you, ya know."

"Really?"

"Really. If you'll let me bring dinner over tonight, I'll sing it for you."

"Okay, Chinese food, 7 P.M., with your guitar."

"Baby, I'm down and I can't wait for you to hear it. Text me today when your class is over."

2 P.M. comes and I get a text. *'What's up?'*

I quickly respond, *'Ya really wanna know??'*

She responds back, *'You PERV! Can't wait to see you!'*

*'Me too!'*

# BEING FAIRYTALE MAN...

**I CAN'T FUNCTION ALL DAY WAITING FOR 7 P.M.**

She buzzes me in, and I stand at her door with my guitar slung over my shoulder. "So, I'm gonna show you what I did for those three days."

I go into the living room and we sit on the floor. She looks at me with pursed lips and her head cocked to the side, cautiously observing me. "So, what *did* you do for three days?"

I tell her about writing "Fairytale Man" and how I was so fucked up and missed her. I smile when she says she wants to hear it. "Promise me you won't laugh. It's my heart and soul poured out in song Kyra. This is for you, babe."

> *You gave something special, so special to me*
> *But I was blind, so blind*
> *Couldn't see, couldn't see*
> *That what you were giving couldn't be taken back*
> *The hurt that I'm feeling*
> *Abilities I lack*
> *I know there's no take backs*
> *But in a perfect world*
> *I'd give it to you, give it to you*
> *And then some, sweet girl*

*And if I gave it, gave it, gave it all back*
*Would you take it, take it, take it all back*
*Cause I'm hurtin, hurtin, hurtin so bad you see*
*Could you give it, give it, just give it to me*
*The chance, babe just one chance*
*To show you, show you I can,*
*Be that, be that, that fairytale man.*
*Cause I took something special that you gave to me*
*You kept it for so long and I finally see*
*So if I gave it, gave it, gave it all back,*
*Would you take it, take it, take it all back*
*Cause I'm lovin, lovin, lovin you all I can*
*Could you just give me, give me, give me the chance*
*I'll show you, show you, that babe*
*I can be, I will be your fairytale man*

When I'm finished singing, she just sits there staring at me, and tears fall from her eyes as she whispers, "Oh my God. You wrote that for me?"

"Every word of it, baby. That's how I express my feelings. See? I was hurting, too." I hang my head because I'm tearing up and I don't want her to see me cry.

She takes my face in her hands and smiles. "That was beautiful, Todd. I think you *are* my fairytale man."

I kiss her nose. "I am, babe. Trust me. I am."

Kyra and I, more or less, work through the taking of her virginity. We're working on our relationship and I think of how there is no girl in the world I would go to these lengths to please. Except Olivia of course—but she's like a mom to me.

Over the next few weeks, we spend every day together. I fucking hate that I'll be going on the road, but she promised me she'll come watch us play as often as she can. I introduced her to the guys, Emily, and Olivia. Everyone loves her which makes me feel like I'm sitting on top of the world. Olivia told me that I'd better not screw this up. She said that she felt Kyra was the one for me. To hear her say that is like the best feeling in the world. I trust her with my life and I know she wouldn't bullshit me. One thing about Olivia and me is that we don't sugarcoat things. If she feels it, she's gonna say it.

The night before we leave, Brenna rears her evil head and I'm forced to tell Kyra about that whole fuckfest. I explain to her that it happened before I met her and I think, at least I hope, she believes me. I even told her that Brenna was claiming that she was pregnant by me. Kyra is pissed and she has every right to be. All I can do is get the paternity test like Olivia said I should and call her bluff.

Tour day leaves me hurting bad. We're going out on the road for months .

Kyra and I are pretty much both emotional wrecks as we watch my bags being loaded onto the bus. I take her hand and we walk around behind the bus where I pull her into my arms.

"Kyra, part of me wants to say fuck it and just stay in Highland Park. I don't wanna leave you."

She backs me up to the bus and kisses me, "Todd, you can't *not* go. It's what you've worked your ass off for. You've got to do it. Besides, you'd hate yourself if you didn't and you know that."

"Baby, I just know that everyone I've ever cared about has left me, and I'm afraid. I'm scared shitless you won't be here when I get back."

She messes with my hair and gives me a silly face. "Olivia's still here. She hasn't left. Todd, I care about you so much and I'll be here for you... but..."

"But what, babe?" I'm scared to hear what she's about to say.

She takes a deep breath. "I'm the one who's scared. What if *you* find someone else? You're the one who has girls chasing you. I'm a nothing."

"Kyra, don't ever, ever, say you're a nothing. You're everything to me, babe. I swear to God there is no other woman who compares to you. I'm gonna prove that to you. You've gotta trust me. Do you give me your word that you trust me?"

She looks down at the ground and I pull her face into mine. "Kyra, before I leave, I fucking need to hear that you trust me because I can't do this unless I know I have your trust and your..."

She looks into my eyes, "My what?"

I shake my head. I've never said this to a girl before and I'm freaking out. "Your love, okay? I need to know I have your love."

She smiles the biggest smile I've ever seen her give. "Wait. Are you saying that you lo–"

"Yes, Kyra, I'm saying that I love you. I love everything about you. I need you so fucking bad. Okay, I said it. I said the L word." I scrunch my face and she jumps into my arms and wraps her legs around me.

"Oh my God! I love you, too. I love you so much!" She's crying, and I'm jumping up and down with her in my arms.

"Okay, baby, so this is serious. I mean, as in we're a couple, right?"

She puts her arms around my neck and tilts her head to look me in the face. "Yes, you butt wipe, we're a couple!"

I walk around to the front of the bus with her in my arms to get Olivia.

"Olivia, I want you to witness this. I've just told this beautiful girl that I love her and guess what?"

Olivia puts her hands on her hips and laughs. "And what? She said she loves ya back? Pfft...I knew it all along..."

Fast forward three weeks...

Little did I know that while we were out on tour, Brian our fucking drummer, would fall off the wagon and take up drugs again. His fiasco almost cost me my relationship with Kyra and our tour. Fucking Brian!

I had a feeling he was using again. I could tell by the way he acted. I never did drugs, but in this business, drugs are like candy. They're everywhere and so many musicians fall into the trap of using. I finally caught him in the act in our hotel room. Fucking ass, just my luck that it was the weekend Kyra came to see us play. Two chicks, lots of coke and Brian was totally wasted. I left Kyra in her room and went to check on Brian. It was one of the worst days in my life. I'd been keeping this from the guys because Brian kept telling me he had it under control, and I wanted so badly to believe him. He didn't, and I put him over Kyra. She fucking left because I came in early the next morning with my boxers on, soaking wet from wrestling Brian in the fucking shower because he was wasted. Try explaining that to a girl who has been waiting on you for hours. A fucked up mess! I'm trying so hard to make this relationship with Kyra work and to show her that I'm a good person, but I fucked that up.

Thank God Olivia ran defense for me and we got that worked out. It wasn't easy, I gotta tell you. Olivia saved my ass and got to Kyra before she hopped a plane back to Chicago.

We worked through everything and Kyra is still with me thank God. I owe her my life for sticking with me. When we got to LA, she came with her mom to watch us play. We'd talked about me meeting her parents, and I know from what she told me that it was gonna be a hard sell with her dad. Her folks are hard core, conservative lawyers and she felt it would be best to have her mom meet me first.

I'd gotten a tattoo with Kyra's name on my chest, above the tattoo I got for my Grammy, in LA and I was pumped to show it to her. It's a beautiful red heart with her name on it. That weekend, Olivia, Mr. H, and Emily, Tommy's wife, also flew out to watch us. Kyra introduced me to Diane, her mom, and she's really cool. I think at first she didn't like me, but I tried my best to convince her that I'm in love with her daughter.

Turns out, Diane told me that she dated a rocker before she married her ultra conservative lawyer husband. I can totally see Diane and Olivia becoming good friends. Diane is younger than Olivia, I think, but still pretty cool.

Our set that night was awesome. There was a huge crowd and I sang "In These Arms" by Bon Jovi to Kyra. I ripped off my shirt, got down on my knees and screamed the words of the song to her. I unveiled my tattoo during the song, and I could feel that Kyra was totally into the song. It was fucking amazing. She was fucking in tears and I was on cloud nine. Diane just sat there smiling shaking her head. Now if I can just convince Kyra's dad that I love her...

# TESTING THE LIMITS OF SKYPE...

**WHILE OUT ON THE ROAD, LET'S FACE IT, GUYS GET HORNY. IT'S A GIVEN. OUR** dicks are our brains. So many guys who have significant others end up cheating because pussy is just thrown in your face on a nonstop basis. You have to be really committed to your relationship to resist the temptation of girls out on the road. I'm finally at a point in my life where those girls don't mean anything to me. At one time, though, I'll admit that I fucked anything I could find, but these days, not at all. I miss Kyra and I want her so fucking bad. We Skype every single night and tonight, the guys are going out on the town. I decide to stay back because I've been working on a new song.

I give them a warning before they leave. "Okay, you fucktards go on without me. I've got something I'm working on. Just remember that the bus leaves at 4 A.M., so you'd better have your asses back here on time. Don't make me come looking for you." I'm pretty confident that Tommy will make sure everyone is back on time because, after all, he's a married man now and Emily would kick his ass if he strayed off the beaten path. Rowdy's married and he's pretty much whipped. His wife is Cajun, and I *know* she would kick his ass from here to China if he fucked around. They all give me their word, no late calls.

I curl up in my bunk, pull out my laptop and get Kyra on Skype. I bite my lip and smile as soon as I see her beautiful face. "Hey, baby. I've missed you. Wanna have some fun tonight?"

She giggles. "Sure. But where are the guys?" I tell her that it's just her and me. The guys have gone out.

"Tommy too?" she asks.

"Yep. All of them. It's just you and me, baby."

I suggest we have a 'session' on Skype and she freaks. "We can't do that!"

I crack up. "Of course we can. Besides, I need you, baby. Let's have Skype sex."

"Whaaaaat?" She gasps.

I laugh. "You heard me. Let's *do it* over Skype. Are you in bed?"

I can tell that she is. "Oh, yeah. Now, I need you to take those clothes off and show me that sexy bra and thong."

She scrunches her face. "Todd, are you serious?"

"As a heart attack, baby. Look."

I've already taken my boxers off *and* I'm naked in my bunk holding myself. "I really need you tonight."

She pants as she looks on the screen at me. "Oh shit. You're gorgeous."

I wink at her. "No, *you* are. Get those damn clothes off."

She peels them off as I watch, and she says, "Are you sure this is legal?"

"Who gives a shit? Lemme see you, Ky."

I see her on her bed in her bra and thong, and it's all I can do to keep from blowing my load.

"Fuck, baby. You're so hot. Now, I want you to touch yourself while I watch."

She squiggles up against the headboard of her bed and looks uncomfortable. I have to coax her. "Come on, baby. It's just us. Do it for me."

She does and I'm slowly stroking myself as I watch her. "Baby, you're so fucking beautiful. Watch me while you do it."

"Oh... Oh...that's such a turn on," she whispers.

"Yeah, now you show me, we get it on, and we have Skype sex. Are ya with me?"

She's working herself and I can tell she's about to come. She's on the brink and I'm there with her.

"Are you sure no one is in the bus?" She gasps.

I laugh. "Positive. I gave Ray a hundred bucks to take a hike. Keep doing what you're doing. I'm almost there." I'm stroking it, and I watch as she pants and her body shakes and shudders. "Oh my God...Oh...Oh!"

I lose my load and it goes all over the screen. I crack up laughing. "Fuck...Oops! Sorry..."

She shakes her head giggling. "Todd, you didn't just do that did you?"

"What does it look like on your end babe? My screen is full of cream."

"I can see spots on my screen. Ewwww!"

I wipe my screen with my boxers and wink at her. "There. Evidence destroyed."

"Wow, that was awesome. I like Skype sex. It's the next best thing to having you here with me. And yes, my screen *was* creamy."

"Fucking-A it is! Damn, baby, you're so damn hot."

We talk for another hour, and I hear the hydraulics of the bus doors open.

I quickly sit up. "Yikes! I gotta put this bad boy up, we've got company." I pull my boxers on, and she pulls the covers over her. I blow her a kiss and disconnect.

The guys are back, and we're off to our next stop. There's total commotion as everyone gets settled in but I'm totally sexually satisfied. I pretend like I'm sleeping, so I don't have to engage in a convo and I get a text from Kyra, *'OMG! I've never done that...I'm gonna sleep so good. I miss you!'*

I text her back, *'Ya wanna do it again tomorrow night?'*

She sends me a happy face and a thumbs up.

I'm happy...hell yeah!

# MEETING THE FAM...

**FAST FORWARD TO THE HOLIDAYS.**

We're back from touring and Kyra has invited me to her folks' house for Thanksgiving. I've told Olivia I won't be coming to her house, and while she's disappointed, she's pumped that I'll be meeting the rest of Kyra's family. I'm so damn nervous, but Kyra puts me at ease. "You already met my Mom. My brothers know who you are, and they can't freakin wait to meet you."

"Yeah, but what about your dad? Does he know about me?"

"I love you. It's gonna be okay, just trust me."

I arrive at the Casa Edwards. It's a huge mansion. I pull into the circular driveway in my Mustang. Her brothers are standing on the driveway motioning me where to park. I get out, take my sunglasses off, squint my eyes, and survey the place. Fucking Taj Mahal. It's a huge brick contemporary home with larger than life double doors and incredible landscaping. The boys walk out to my car and are ogling over it. "Wow! Your car is sick!"

I extend my hand. "Hi, I'm Todd."

"Hi ,Todd. I'm Landon, this is Logan. You're so freaking awesome!"

I laugh, "Well, let's just hope your dad thinks so."

"Word." Landon fist pumps and laughs.

They lead me into the house and Diane is busy in the kitchen. She's just as nice as she was in L.A. She wipes her hands on her apron and smiles when she sees me, "Hey, Todd, welcome to our home! I sent Kyra to the store, but she'll be right back. Lamar is in his study, he'll be out soon."

I'm assuming Lamar is 'daddy' and I nervously shake my head. Diane motions me to sit at the bar in the kitchen. "Can I get you a beer or a drink?"

I smile politely. "Thanks, Diane, a beer would be great."

Landon jumps in front of her. "I'll get it." I laugh and point at the two of them. "How do you even tell you guys apart? I mean, you look exactly alike."

"It's easy. I'm Landon, and I'm the hot one."

I rub my chin and smile. "Okay, so is there a birthmark or something that will make me know the difference between Landon and Logan because both of you are pretty good looking."

About that time, Kyra comes through the door with bags of groceries and she squeals when she sees me. She hands her bags off to her brothers and jumps into my arms. I don't want to have a make out fest, but I feel a twinge in my crotch when I see her. Her eyes light up. "Babe!"

I give her a kiss and set her down. I don't want to seem overly excited but I swear to God, I'm so happy to see her. Diane laughs. "Kyra, your father is in his study. Why don't you go get him?"

Kyra points at me, grins and says, "I'll be right back."

Before long, she's leading a man who is large, distinguished, and very intimidating. She's smiling as she introduces us. "Daddy, this is my boyfriend Todd O'Malley. Todd, this is my daddy, Lamar."

We exchange cordial handshakes, and I can tell 'daddy' isn't too keen on me. I dressed 'normally', intentionally covering my tats and even wore a nice pair of jeans. I feel his eyes assessing me.

"Nice to meet you, son. Kyra has told us nice things about you," he coolly says.

Landon pipes up. "Dad, for God's sake, he's a freaking rock star!"

He shakes his head unknowingly and holds his hand up. "Okay, Landon, thanks for the trivia."

Fucking trivia? Holy shit, this isn't good.

Lamar, a.k.a. 'daddy', grills me about my whole fucking life. I knew this was gonna be different, but Jesus. This man is raking me over the coals. I know his daughter means the world to him, but Jesus H. Christ just please get me through this.

Kyra comes to stand beside me and weaves her arm into mine. "Daddy, Todd is just back from touring with his band, Avenue. They have songs on the radio."

Lamar chuckles. "Songs I haven't heard sweetie. Your mom and brothers have, but I'm stuck on classical music, you know that."

We all bullshit, for lack of a better word, until Lamar announces that he has to go into his study and do some work. He must be pretty important because who the fuck works on Thanksgiving Day?

I sit at the bar in the kitchen and have offered to help Diane, but she resists and insists I'm a guest. Kyra sits in my lap, and I swear to God, the south is rising. I have my arm around her, rubbing her shoulder. She turns to face me, bites her lip and moves around on my lap whispering, "I can't wait until we're alone."

Deep down I'm thinking with 'daddy' in the house, that ain't gonna happen. I kiss her ear and whisper back, "Baby, you have no idea how bad I wanna be alone with you."

Diane announces Thanksgiving dinner with a little bell and a smile. We're ushered into this grand formal dining room. The whole house is ultra-contemporary. The dining room is void of the happy feeling I get when I go to Olivia's house.

The walls are white with a dark grey ceiling. There's this fucking huge, black dining room table with twelve white leather chairs surrounding it, and a dark marble floor. Something about the atmosphere in this house is not very inviting. I can't really explain it, but I'm not getting a warm fuzzy feeling at all. I miss the welcoming feeling that I get when I'm at the Harper house. Olivia has this way of making everyone feel welcome and loved. This scene is anything but. Diane is doing her best to make this fun, but Jesus, I ain't feeling the love. Lamar is dressed in nice pants and a starched dress shirt and sits at the head of the table. I wonder if this mother fucker ever just breaks out into a natural smile. He looks fake and I can't get a good read on him. Diane looks at him and smiles like a Stepford Wife. I can't believe I'm doing this. You gotta know how much Kyra means to me because I'd be adios-ing this for anyone but her. Lamar grabs a bottle of Cristal from the champagne bucket and pops the cork, pouring our glasses. No toast like Mr. H, just pouring the shit into a glass. I look to Kyra, and she toasts me then whispers in my ear, "To us."

Lamar makes us all stand while he says a blessing and I can tell this poor mother fucker was coaxed into doing this. He's out of his element. I open my eyes and see Diane smiling, squeezing Lamar's hand. I make it through dinner, and I jump up to help Diane clear the table with Kyra. "Oh, absolutely not, Todd. Kyra and I have this." She waves her hand smiling. "You go have a cigar with Lamar."

Lamar looks over the top of his glasses and smiles a fake smile. "Todd, let's go have a stogie in my study, shall we?" The twins get up and follow us but Lamar stops them, "You've already gotten to know Todd, so why don't you let us get to know each other?" The look on his face makes the boys scatter, and I'm a bit perplexed and now uncomfortable. Is he really such a dominating person?

Lamar leads the way to his study. The sound of our shoes walking in unison on the dark wood floor reverberates in my ear. Two ornately carved, dark wood, contemporary double doors with huge silver circular handles open as Lamar motions me to sit. I hear a click, and I turn back to see the deadbolt turn. We're fucking locked in. Lamar smirks and points. "It locks on its own. It's programmed that way. Not to worry."

I'm blown away because this room is as traditional as they get. There is dark wood paneling, built-ins with tons of books, large dark leather chairs, a carved wooden desk, and a fucking six foot knight in armor standing in the corner staring at me.

Lamar notices me checking it out. "I gave Diane full reign over the decor of the house, but this room, my office is *my* sanctuary. The knight? He's one of the things I found in Europe. Diane despises it, but this room is off limits to the female species, so I really don't give a damn." He smiles as he moves to sit behind his desk and with his hand, motions me to sit in one of the leather chairs facing his desk. We talk briefly about Kyra. He tells me shit about her I already know but I act like it's the first time I've heard it. Does he think Kyra and I don't even talk?

He leans over his desk and lowers his glasses. "Kyra is just about finished with her master's degree. She's hoping to get a seat on the Chicago Stock Exchange. I didn't know if you knew that."

I shake my head. "I did know that, sir. She's a very smart woman, and

I know without a doubt she'll get there. Sooner than later, I'd guess."

He exhales from a puff on his cigar. "She's been distracted lately. I'm not sure if your fling has anything to do with this, but her mother and I feel that she needs to focus on her studies."

He swirls around in his chair with his cigar, grabs the remote control, points it at the TV, revealing a shit eating grin and remarks, "I like movies. This is one I just got." He blows a smoke ring and clears his throat.

I'm fucking caught off guard. It's the video of Brenna, Red, and me. Lamar leans back in his chair with his hands behind his head and turns his back to me. There is silence in the room as I look away from the screen and down at the floor. I hear Brenna talking in the video; narrating the whole fucking scene blow by blow. I hear her snide laugh, and the bile is rising in my throat, "So, Kyra's dad, I guess you're wondering where your daughter is. Are ya wondering why she wasn't there with us?" Then there is laughing. "She got sloppy seconds. That's why. Bahahaha!"

I stand up and slam my fist on the desk. "This is bullshit!"

Lamar turns around and looks at me over his fucking glasses. "Really? You think it's bullshit? I think you're trash and don't deserve to be seeing my daughter. Your actions seem to speak louder than your words, son."

We have a stare down, and I get in his face. "Look, this happened long before I met Kyra. It's an attempt to extort and I'm suing this woman."

Lamar smiles a devious smile. "Just the response I expected. Let's bring up litigation. I hear it every day."

I try and explain myself, Kyra, and the way I feel about her but he's not getting it. The conversation has gone from bad to worse.

He points the remote at the TV, gets up, and stretches. "I think I've seen enough, how about you, Todd?"

I walk to the door, turn the handle and it's locked. "I'd like you to let me out, sir. I've had enough."

He laughs a creepy laugh. "Sorry, of course I'll let you out, and I hope this viewing will make you see that Kyra is far above you. It would probably be best if you just leave."

He points at the door, "By the way, happy Thanksgiving."

My heart is beating out of my chest and there's a ringing in my ears. I exit the office and try to find the nearest way out. I've gotta get the hell out of here, but I can't leave without talking to Kyra. I walk into the kitchen to see her and Diane laughing while loading the dishwasher. When she sees me she smiles. "So did you and Daddy have a nice visit?"

I smile but my heart is aching as I take her into my arms, lift her face up and kiss her nose. "Yeah, baby we did. Look, I gotta go."

She's stunned. "Go? Why? It's Thanksgiving."

I pull her into me, kiss her forehead and whisper in her ear, "Something came up. I'll call you later."

I walk to the front door and she follows me, pulling my arm. "Wait. What's wrong, babe?"

I try and reassure her. "Nothing. Something with the band, that's all. Everything's good."

We walk out to my car. I just need to leave. She leans in my window. "Can't they do without you until tomorrow? I don't understand."

"Look, baby, I'll call you later."

She knows something's wrong. "Todd, what happened with you and Daddy? I know something's wrong. Don't leave me like this."

I put my head on the steering wheel before replying. "Ky, Brenna sent the video to your dad. I gotta think things out. Look, I'm no good for you. I want you so bad, but baby, I don't know..." I start my car and begin to back out of the driveway.

She yells out, "Okay, do it to me again! Leave! Take the chicken shit way out, Todd. Fuck you!" She flips me off. I want to put my car back into drive, pull up and take her into my arms but I gotta get the hell out of here.

# Can This Relationship
# Be Saved?

**I PEEL OUT AND FIND PEACE SPEEDING DOWN THE FREEWAY. TEARS ARE** streaming down my face. Fuck! The last time I cried was when my Grammy died. I only cry when there is a death, so I guess I just died. Everything I love dies, so this is just how my life goes. I spot a liquor store that's open, and I pull into the parking lot. I stare inside and try to decide whether or not I want a bottle. I decide to call Olivia instead. The sound of her voice makes me break down.

"Honey, what's wrong? Are you okay?"

I blurt out, "No, I'm fucking not okay. Are you in town?"

"Yes, we stayed here. The kids are here, too. Wanna come over?"

I don't want company. "No, I'm just gonna head over to Grammy's. I'll be okay. Call ya tomorrow."

Olivia's not buying it. "Todd, I know you and something's wrong. Look, give me twenty minutes, and I'll be there."

"I don't want to fuck up your holiday. Really I'm okay, I swear. I'm almost to Grammy's. I'm just gonna drink and get twisted off. I'm good."

In a matter of minutes she pulls up at Grammy's. I walk out to meet her as she gets out of her car and she holds her arms out. "Come here. I know something's wrong." Just seeing her there with her arms spread for me makes me feel so fucking good. I hug her and she holds me so tight. "Olivia, Brenna sent the video to Kyra's dad. He played it for me in his office. It was just him and me. That's why I left."

"Oh, honey, I'm so sorry..."

She holds me close, and I hang on to her. I lose it and I'm fucking crying like a baby. I wipe my nose with my hand and shake my head. "Fuck. I'm done with this. Every time I try to love, someone leaves me. I'm just gonna go back to being my old self. It's much simpler that way."

Olivia takes my face into her hands and she has a puzzled look on her face, "That makes no sense. I'm sorry but you're full of shit. My Todd doesn't talk like that."

I go into detail about the situation in Lamar's study and she shivers. "I don't know what to say except my heart hurts for you, hon. You and Kyra need to talk about this and decide what's more important—your relationship or what her father thinks. It sounds as though Diane is on board with things, right?"

I shrug my shoulders. "Well, yeah, because Diane doesn't know about the video. At least I don't think she does."

While Olivia and I are talking, I get a text from Kyra. *I'm at your house. Where are you?*

I show the screen to Olivia, and she pushes it back toward me. "Tell her where you are. Tell her you want her to come over here." I look at her and take a deep breath.

She messes up my hair. "That is what you want, isn't it?"

I shake my head and hold my arms out to her. "Lady bug, you know me way better than I know myself. Yeah, that's exactly what I want."

She gets her keys out of her purse and winks at me. "I don't wanna be the third wheel, so I'm gonna head back to the house. You and Kyra are more than welcome to come hang out. You know that right?"

I give her a thumbs up. "I do know that, babe."

I'm texting Kyra as I walk Olivia to her car. *Come to my Grammy's house*

I close the car door once Olivia gets in. "I'll call ya manana. Maybe with good news."

She blows me a kiss, and before she drives off, she points at me, "I'm counting on good news! Love you!"

Kyra texts me back, *On my way. Be there in 15.'*

# IT'S TIME TODD...
## VOICES FROM ABOVE

**I GO ROAM AIMLESSLY FROM ROOM TO ROOM, REMEMBERING THE GOOD** times I had here in this house with my grandparents. I stop outside Grammy's bedroom and realize how much I miss her. Something calls me into the room and I go lie on her bed. I pull the covers to my nose. Her scent is still on the bedspread, and I think back to the awesome hugs she used to give me. I stare at her dresser, looking at her perfume bottles and my eyes go to her jewelry box. It's the one I gave her when I was just a little kid. I haven't cleaned out any of the stuff in her room since she died because it just didn't seem right.

Emily and Kyra moved into the house for the summer before we left out on tour. Emily had suggested I wait for the right time to sort through things and I'm glad she did. I open the jewelry box and sitting on the top red velvet shelf is her engagement ring. Sitting next to it is an old photo of her and Grampy when they got married. They look so young and happy. I pick the picture up and smile.

Grammy told me the story of how my Grampy proposed to her at the county fair and I remember she cried with joy as she shared that. She told me Grampy didn't have enough money to buy her a ring, so his mother gave him her own mother's ring. That makes the ring in my hand really old. I suddenly feel Grammy nudging me on my shoulder, telling me that I need to make a commitment to the one I love. I hold the ring in my hand

and it's as if she's telling me, "Todd, son it's time. You need to take that girl as your wife."

I swear to God I've never felt her presence as much as I do right now. Maybe she's right. I love Kyra with all my heart—that I know.

I look out the upstairs window and see lights from Kyra's car pulling up in the driveway as I put Grammy's ring in my pocket.

Kyra knocks on the door and as soon as I open it she's in my arms. "Todd, look...I..."

I put my fingers on her lips. "Shhhh, Kyra, we've got a shitload of things to work through. I know that. I've fucked up so many times, and I have a lot of proving myself to do. I don't know if I can do it, but one thing I *do* know is that I love you, and I don't wanna live without you." I take her hand and we walk into the music room where I sit her on the piano bench.

"What are you doing?" she asks.

My hands are sweating and shaking as I drop to my knee. My voice cracks, "Kyra, I love you with all my heart. I don't want to live, no make that I *can't*, live without you. I'll do whatever it takes to make your folks realize that I'm the one for you. I swear to God. Will you accept this ring and be my wife?"

I take her shaking left hand and put the ring on her finger. It fits perfect, and I can feel Grammy and my mom smiling down on me.

Kyra is gasping and her body is heaving as she cries. I'm thinking, just praying that she's not gonna tell me to get fucked. When suddenly I see her smile and put her hand over her mouth. "Oh my God..."

I look up at her with a painful look on my face., "Baby! Is that a yes or a no? I'm dying here."

She pushes me down on the floor and lies on top of me. "It's a yes. Yes, yes, yes! When did you get this ring? Oh my GOD, it's beautiful."

I hold her hand and rub the ring on her finger. "It belonged to my Grammy and her mother in law before that."

She holds her hand out and stares at the ring. "It's the most beautiful ring I've ever seen and the fact that you gave me something so close to your family..."

I take her hair and pull it back from her face. "Ky, the ring is the simple part. The rest ain't gonna be easy. After today, it's gonna get really complicated and I just want us to be together on this. Once you say yes, it's forever, okay?"

She gives me her pinkie finger, and I add mine, "What's this?" I ask.

"Now we pinky swear. Once we do this, it can't be broken. It's forever."

She traces her finger over my lips and kisses me as she whispers, "Are you my Fairytale Man, Todd?"

I smile and answer, kissing her between each word, "Angel, I am your Fairytale Man. Forever."

~The End~

Follow Todd and Kyra in the 3rd book of the Out of the Box Series, Out of the Box Everlasting due out in early 2015.

# ACKNOWLEDGEMENTS

## People who make a difference in my life

FIRST AND FOREMOST, MY FAMILY IS AT THE TOP OF THE LIST OF acknowledgements. I could not do this without the support and encouragement they give me. Do I neglect them? Do I slack on my household duties? Do I forget important dates? Am I the worlds worst at calling my kids and grandkids? Is my husband left on his own at night to fend for himself fixing dinner? Guilty on all counts, yet they still come to my events and cheer me on.

I love you all!

Next on the list is a woman who is a rock goddess in the beta reading department and there just aren't enough adjectives to describe her talents. She's also become a dear friend and I am so blessed that she continues to read my manuscripts. She doesn't cut me any slack and is brutally honest, but I respect and appreciate that. Tbird, you're still my hero and I love my T-time!

To my CLS sisters – what can I say? The love and support that abounds in this diverse group of twenty five amazing ladies (who are equally amazing authors) is astounding. There isn't a day when I don't connect with them. Even though we are separated geographically, there isn't a day when we don't chat online and believe me I treasure the friendships I've made with you all. #PTTP ladies..I love you all!

Diane Rinella – you are officially my partner in crime. For the record,

I'll be your table buddy at book signings any time anywhere. I love our phone convos on my daily commute home from work and I adore you. Your room is always ready at casa Theriot! I know you love the heat and humidity in my city....

To my street team – Jennifer's Jewels, you ladies ROCK! These diamonds shine for me on the streets of Facebook, Twitter Google + and other social media relentlessly on a daily basis. I call, they answer and they do it so well! Day after day they pimp me and there are no words to express my gratitude. Thank you gals for all you do...Shine on! #TeamTheriot

Tanya Watt recently took over my website duties. She does my book trailers, sends out blasts and is a dream to work with. I looooove her creative mind! She also prodded me into blogging by giving me step by step instructions. Thank you Tanya for making me step Out of the Box..☺

Stephanie Sakry – you are the BEST PA ever! 'No problem' is her motto.. When I need something at the 11th hour, she handles it and makes it seem effortless. She's an amazing person and I'm so lucky! Good PA's are hard to come by and I was blessed....

I Love ya Steph!

I have to give a heartfelt mention to a multi talented musician and dear friend by the name of Mark Odom. Mark took my lyrics to Fairytale Man and made them come alive in song. When he sent me his recording, I was brought to tears...He recorded two versions of the song and I'm so honored that he did this for me. I encourage you all to check out his website and witness the talents of this amazing man. I love you Mark!!

Now on to Team Toccata:

One of my CLS sisters (and fellow author) RE Hargrave gave me the suggestion for the title – which took my breath away. We chatted in our group and I mentioned what the novella was about and once she typed the words Toccata Obbligato I was in awe. Adding Serenading Kyra completed the title. Many thanks RE ....I heart you.

JC Clarke with Grafix Momma is the awesome cover designer for TOSK. I sent her the story line, a physical description of my characters and she blew me away with her design. Wow! Just Wow! Thanks JC for putting a brand to my book. I can't quit looking at the cover. *handovermouth*

To my editor, Crystal Marie from Little House of Edits...thank you once again for squeezing me in at the last minute and while you were sick to boot!

For proofreading, I used Anne Duellman at White Wolf Proofing Services, author PJ Fiala and Tiffany Tillman with Redhead Book Services These busy ladies also found time to fit me in at the 11th hour. Many thanks ladies!

The formatting guru is Courtney Nuckels with Clean Teen Publishing who makes this whole process come to life with her creative formatting touches. I love our online convos where we bounce ideas back and forth. With a play on ideas, a few key strokes and a "be right back" she produces an amazing final product.

So, as you can see, there are a lot of people who make my world so special. It is with much love and appreciation that I salute you all!

## The links to these talented folks are listed below:

https://www.facebook.com/Grafixmommauk

https://www.facebook.com/AuthorTanyaWatt

https://www.facebook.com/littlehouseofedits

https://www.facebook.com/pages/White-Wolf-Proofing-Services/361039850716195

https://www.facebook.com/redheadbookservices/info

https://www.facebook.com/cleanteenpublishing

Spotify Playlist for Toccata Obbligato ~Serenading Kyra
Toccata Obbligato~Serenading Kyra Playlist

Website for Mark Odom:
http://www.markonguitar.com

# ABOUT THE AUTHOR

**JENNIFER THERIOT LIVES IN THE GREAT STATE OF TEXAS.**

She is married with three grown children and three grandkids; all of whom she adores...

By day, she's a number cruncher—working as a CFO for a real estate investment firm. She writes at night and on weekends and her passion for writing lies with second chance romance.

In her spare time you'll find her curled up on the beach reading romance and listening to music—her admitted addictions.

**Connect with Jennifer:**
http://www.jennifertheriot.com
https://www.facebook.com/JenniferTheriotAuthor
https://twitter.com/JenTheRiot?lang=en

WHEN LIFE GIVES YOU A
SECOND CHANCE,
EMBRACE IT LIKES THERE'S
NO TOMORROW.

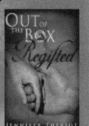

THE OUT OF THE BOX SERIES IS A STORY
OF SHARED PASSION AND SHARED JOY.
JENNIFER THERIOT HAS WRITTEN A
COMPELLING BOOK ABOUT WHAT
HAPPENS WHEN TWO PEOPLE FIND NEW
LIFE AND NEW LOVE FOR THEMSELVES
AND FOR THOSE AROUND THEM.

Made in the USA
Middletown, DE
21 April 2015